LETTERS HOME from KENYA

Marcia S. Gresko

BLACKBIRCH PRESS, INC.
WOODBRIDGE, CONNECTICUT

Published by Blackbirch Press, Inc.
260 Amity Road
Woodbridge, CT 06525

First Edition

e-mail: staff@blackbirch.com
Web site: www.blackbirch.com

Printed in Singapore

10 9 8 7 6 5 4 3 2 1

Library of Congress Cataloging-in-Publication Data

Gresko, Marcia S.
Kenya / by Marcia S. Gresko.
p. cm. — (Letters home from . . .)
Includes bibliographical references and index.
Summary: Describes some of the sights and experiences on a trip to Kenya, including visits to Nairobi, a Masai boma, and the Masai Mara Game Reserve.
ISBN 1-56711-405-9
1. Kenya—Juvenile literature. [1. Kenya—Description and travel.] I. Title. II. Series.
DT433.522.G74 1999 99-27024
967.62—dc21 CIP
AC

TABLE OF CONTENTS

Arrival in . . .

Nairobi

Jambo (hello) from Kenya! Yesterday, we flew over to the east coast of Africa and landed in Nairobi—Kenya's capital.

According to the guidebook, Kenya is about as big as the state of Texas. It has every kind of scenery on the planet! There are silvery beaches and scorching deserts. There are icy glaciers and extinct volcanoes. We'll also get to stand on two sides of the world! The equator passes right through the middle of Kenya—that's what divides the earth into the Northern and Southern hemispheres.

As we circled the airport, the pilot told us to look out our windows for a great view. Below us, zebras, giraffes, and rhinos grazed in Nairobi National Park, right next to the airport. I was glad I had brought my binoculars!

Modern Nairobi

Yesterday, we toured modern Nairobi. It was hard to believe that 100 years ago the city was a cattle watering hole!

Now Nairobi is the business and political center of Kenya. Surrounding our hotel are high-rise offices, banks, and government buildings like Parliament, where the country's laws are made. There are also universities, museums, peaceful parks, churches, and mosques. Most Kenyans are Christians. A small percentage are Muslims, mostly descendants of African peoples and the Arab traders who controlled the country for nearly 500 years.

When we left our hotel for the city market today, the brightly painted mini-buses, called matatus, were already jammed with people!

Mosques

Everyone was going to work in Nairobi's factories and businesses. Nairobi is one of the fastest growing cities in Africa. Every year, thousands of Kenyans come here from rural areas to look for jobs. Many are unable to find work. They live in crowded slums without running water or electricity.

At the market, we joined a crowd of people. We passed stalls crammed with baskets, wood carvings, and fancy beaded jewelry. Other stalls were piled high with fruits and vegetables grown in the fertile farmland just outside the city.

Farming is very important in Kenya. Crowded Nairobi makes you forget that most Kenyans live and work on small family farms in the countryside.

Nairobi—Ethnic Groups

Last evening we visited the bomas of Kenya in a suburb of Nairobi. A boma is a traditional settlement.

Kenya is home to about 40 different ethnic groups. Each has its own language, religion, festivals, and culture. The largest ethnic group in Kenya is the Kikuyu. Others are the Luo, Luhya, and Kalenjin. Some groups, like the Kikuyu and the Luo, have adopted many Western ways. Other groups, such as the Masai and the Turkana, have mostly kept their traditional lifestyles. Though many of Kenya's ethnic groups occupy their own homelands in the countryside, in Nairobi they work and live as neighbors.

Though they have differences, Kenya's ethnic groups also have many similarities. Family life is very important. Marriage, birth, and coming of age ceremonies are major events.

Tribal dancers

Masai

Last night, outside the Masai boma, we talked to a young moran, or warrior. Though they are a small ethnic group, the Masai are well-known for their bravery. Not very long ago, it was customary for a Masai boy to prove he was a man by killing a lion with only a spear as his weapon. Even today, the Masai stand guard over their herds of cattle armed only with shields and spears. The Masai shield and crossed spears pictured in the center of Kenya's flag represent the country's defense of freedom.

Young Masai warrior

Serengeti Plain

The drive southwest from Nairobi to Masai Mara Game Reserve was like being in a wildlife film. The Masai Mara is part of neighboring Tanzania's huge Serengeti Plain, an area bigger than the state of Connecticut. Outside our window stretched the savanna, an area of rolling grasslands. Scattered, flat-topped acacia trees dotted the landscape. And elephants, ostriches, giraffes, and zebras grazed peacefully in the distance. I can hardly wait to see them up close!

Outside the entrance to the reserve was a Masai village.

Ostrich on Serengeti Plain

Balloon safari

Masai Customs

The Masai are nomadic herders and concentrate on finding grazing land for their cattle. They worship one god whom they believe gave them cattle as a gift.

Masai homes are igloo-shaped huts made from branches plastered with cattle dung. When the dung dries, it's as strong as cement and doesn't smell at all! The village is surrounded by a thornbush fence, keeping it safe from wild animals.

As Masai children get older, they are expected to help the village. Boys learn everything about cattle. Girls learn how to cook and clean house.

Both girls and boys have coming-of-age ceremonies. Girls have them at 12 years old, and boys have them at about 16. After their ceremony, girls can marry. A year later, the boys become senior warriors and can marry.

Women in Masai village

Traditional Masai dance

Safari—Masai Mara Game Reserve

Our safari began yesterday! The word safari means "journey" in Kiswahili. In the past, safaris were hunting trips, and travelers brought back skins, heads, and tusks as trophies. Today, the only shots taken are with a camera.

According to our guide, Kenya leads all other African nations in protecting its wildlife. Hunting has been banned. The Masai Mara is one of 40 game reserves and national parks where animals can roam free.

Kenya's animals are a national treasure and a major attraction. Nearly a million tourists like us visit Kenya from all over the world each year, mostly to see the wildlife.

Sadly, not everyone values the animals. Many parks suffer from poaching—that's the killing of protected animals for their skins, horns, or tusks.

Safari vehicle

Masai women

Mara River

The Masai Mara was like a giant zoo without cages. There were animals everywhere! Lions lurked in the tall grass, elephants gave themselves showers at watering holes, and hippos dozed in the swamps. But the highlight of our trip to the Mara was our view of the annual wildebeest migration. In the summer, millions of these odd-looking animals move north from the Serengeti in Tanzania to the Mara in search of pastures. What a sight!

Hippos in morning light

Hippos in the Mara River

Amboseli National Park

We traveled southeast of the Masai Mara Game Reserve to Amboseli National Park. Our driver explained that in game reserves, people like the Masai can graze their animals and can kill predators if they are attacked. In a national park, the entire area is set aside for the wildlife and the natural environment.

Elephants

Cheetah

Amboseli Serena Lodge

Elephant

Morning is the best time to see animals in action, so we've been starting out early. By noon, it's very hot and many animals are resting. But one afternoon we saw a cheetah, the fastest animal on earth, sprint at 70 miles an hour to bring down an antelope! Our driver explained that many of the animals in the larger parks are changing their habits. Many animals hunt after the tourists have headed home. He told us that he couldn't get any closer because he didn't want to scare the cheetah from its kill.

We've also seen plenty of the biggest (and one of the smartest) animals on earth—elephants. Elephants like company and are usually seen in herds. They need a lot of food and water, so herds are always on the move—and you don't want to be in their way when they are!

Wild Animals

We got pretty close to some lions today. Our driver said that it was safe to do because the lions had eaten their fill of a wildebeest they'd killed. After stuffing itself on wildebeest meat, a lion will not kill for several days.

Not everyone in our group thinks that the simba (Kiswahili for lion) deserves to be called the king of beasts. Our driver says that lions are lazy and not nearly as smart as leopards! The female lionesses do all the work. They raise the cubs and do all the hunting. Then the male lions eat first! But I think the male lion looks like a king with its huge mane. He certainly sounds like a king with his powerful roar.

Wildebeest

Male African lion

Around the remains of a zebra, scavenger birds like vultures and huge, weird-looking Marabou storks pick the scraps. The Marabous are taller than I am, and their wingspan is 10 to 12 feet wide!

No matter where we go in the park, there's a view of Mt. Kilimanjaro. Even though the mountain seems so close, it's actually in northern Tanzania, on Kenya's border. Our driver says it looks so close because it's so tall—the tallest mountain in Africa.

Wild Animals

According to Masai legend, an angry elephant pulled the rhinoceros's horn into its funny shape. Sadly, that funny-shaped horn has caused the rhino to be hunted nearly to extinction. Poachers kill rhinos and sell their horns. Some people believe that powdered rhino horns have healing powers. Others value the horns as handles for knives. Though they have been around since prehistoric times, rhinos are now one of the most endangered animals in the world. There are fewer than 500 rhinos left in Kenya! The government has taken bold steps to save them. Special teams of rangers have been assigned to guard them and this seems to be working.

Black rhinoceros and egret

Rothchild's giraffe

One of Kenya's three kinds of giraffe, the Rothschild's giraffe, also faced extinction. But unlike the rhinos who were being killed by poachers, the giraffes were being killed mostly by farmers. As Kenya's population grew, people began to settle and farm the land where the giraffes lived. When the giraffes knocked down their fences and destroyed their crops, the farmers killed them. Relocating the Rothschild's giraffes has saved them.

One animal that is definitely not endangered is the zebra. They're everywhere!

So are the vervet monkeys, and they're very curious. Several of them live near our lodge, and they're always looking for hand-outs!

Wild Animals

Today was our last day on safari, so it was a treat to see so many different kinds of animals!

We saw three really big herbivores (animals that eat plants). Herbivores often become dinner for carnivores—animals like lions and cheetahs that eat meat.

First we saw some buffalo. I was surprised when our driver told us that they're the most dangerous animals to humans in all of Africa! Because of their long, curving horns and their unpredictable behavior, it's better not to surprise them. We stayed clear, but the egrets on their backs were happy to hitch a ride. They snack on the insects stirred up as the buffalo move through the plains.

Buffalo

Some of the biggest grazers we saw were the hippos. Our driver said that a full-grown human can sit inside a hippo's mouth! Hippos spend most of their time wallowing in shallow water. Their ears, eyes, and noses are placed high on their heads so that they remain above water even when the rest of their bodies are submerged.

Later, as we said good-bye and asante sana (thank you very much) to our driver, we all felt very lucky to have shared these last few days with Kenya's beautiful animals.

Embu

We stopped in Embu, on the southeastern slopes of Mt. Kenya.

The highlight of our stop was a performance of traditional Embu songs and dances. Singing is one way Kenya's peoples recall favorite stories and record important historical events. Dances are accompanied by clapping hands, stamping feet, playing fancy horns, and beating large drums called ngoma. Our guide explained that most dances have some religious purpose, such as asking the spirits for a good harvest or to bring rain. Most Kenyans believe in one supreme being and in many spirits that influence events. These spirits can live almost anywhere—inside a rock, tree, or stream. The belief that spirits live in objects is called animism.

For part of the festivities, skilled dancers performed on stilts. Embu children spend hours playing on stilts before they can learn the complicated dance steps.

Embu drummer

Mt. Kenya

We got up at dawn today to get a view of soaring Mt. Kenya before it was covered in clouds. What a sight!

Mt. Kenya is the highest mountain in Kenya and the second-highest in Africa. It is really an extinct volcano with glaciers on its slopes and twin, snow-covered peaks at the top. It's hard to believe that it sits on the equator.

According to a Kikuyu legend, Mt. Kenya was built by the god, Ngai. The mountain and the land around it were given to the Ngai people for all time.

Mt. Kenya

Baragoi

We headed north to the city of Baragoi.

On our way we stopped to do some bird-watching. When you're on safari seeing huge elephants and speedy cheetahs, you forget that Kenya has an incredible number of other kinds of animals like birds and insects. Our guide told us that there are 600 different kinds of butterflies alone!

At Lake Bogoria, we saw thousands of flamingos. The lake is very salty so almost nothing lives in it. The lake has boiling hot springs and geysers, too.

Street in Baragoi

Rainbow over Lake Bogoria

Baragoi itself is a small rural town. Life in Kenya's rural towns and villages centers around farming and raising livestock. There are few modern conveniences. Families live in small houses with thatched roofs, walls made of mud, and dirt floors. There is usually no electricity or running water. Cooking is done over small fires.

We had a traditional dinner of ugali (a thick corn meal porridge) and vegetables or meat. Then we sat as the town's people gathered to talk, tell stories, or play games. We watched a lively soccer game. Soccer is Kenya's national sport. Sometimes the government brings in an electric generator and projector to show movies.

Most people go to bed early, so we did too.

Turkana People

We're continuing our adventures further north to Lake Turkana. That's Kenya's largest lake.

The Turkana people and several other groups live along the lake. Because this is such an isolated area, the Turkana have kept most of their age-old customs.

Like the Masai, the Turkana are mostly nomads. Daily life is centered around caring for their herds of animals. Children usually have the responsibility of taking care of the sheep and goats. Older boys and men herd cattle and camel in the desert scrub. Women and girls make the huts, gather firewood and water, and care for children.

Family hut, Lake Turkana

The villagers also fish in Lake Turkana. But the lake is filled with hippos, the largest congregation of Nile crocodiles in the world, and many kinds of poisonous snakes. Needless to say, fishing around here is a bit dangerous!

A Turkana homestead is called an awi. An awi includes a man, his wife or wives, and their children. Married sons, their wives, and children also live in the awi.

Traditional Turkana dress is very colorful. Men often cover part of their hair with mud. Then they paint it blue and decorate it with feathers. They wrap a bright blanket around their bodies and over one shoulder. Women wear lots of beaded and metal jewelry. Different beads and designs stand for certain events, such as marriage.

Samburu People, Great Rift Valley

Our recent stops—Baragoi and lakes Bogoria and Turkana—were all in parts of the Great Rift Valley. According to the guidebook, this huge, more than 4,000-mile-long split in the earth was formed by earthquakes and volcanic eruptions in prehistoric times. The rift begins in the Middle East and cuts its way through Africa to Mozambique in the south. The Great Rift Valley is so large that astronauts can see it on their space flights!

Because the long, wide valley covers such a large area, it is home to several peoples including the Turkana, Pokot, Rendille, and Samburu.

Sunset over Samburu Reserve

Young Samburu girl

Young Samburu warrior

The Great Rift Valley

The Samburu make their homes in the well-watered highlands around Mt. Nyiru, on whose peaks they believe their god lives. The pleasant countryside is lush with meadows, trees, and tall grasses. The Samburu herd cattle and raise crops.

Our guide explained that the Samburu and the Masai are related to one another and share the same language and many of the same traditions. Customs such as coming-of-age ceremonies are celebrated with feasting and merrymaking, as is the birth of a child. Samburu girls usually have their marriages arranged by their parents. A Samburu man must pay his future wife's parents a bride price, usually a certain number of cattle and sheep.

Western Kenya

We're leaving Kenya tomorrow, so I'll probably be showing you our scrapbook before you get this letter!

We've spent our last few days exploring the sights in the western part of the country. The mild climate and fertile soil make this the most populated part of Kenya. Farms dot the countryside and fishing villages perch on the banks of Lake Victoria. The lake is on the border of Kenya and Tanzania. It's the largest lake in Africa and the second-largest lake in the world.

Western Kenya

Fence line,
Cherangani Hills

Baobab trees

Today we visited the Kakamega Forest Reserve, Kenya's tropical rainforest. It was beautiful and very wet! Many rainforest animals are found nowhere else in Kenya. We stood very still and watched a blue monkey and a bush-tailed porcupine go about their business. There are also more than 125 different kinds of trees in the forest.

One tree that we've seen in many different parts of the country is the baobab, Kenya's most famous tree. It looks like it's growing with its roots sticking up in the air! People use its trunk, bark, leaves, fruit, and seeds for many things from canoes to medicine.

Tomorrow we'll travel east to Nairobi to board our plane back home. It will be hard to say kwaheri (good-bye) to Kenya.

Glossary

Animism belief that spirits live in objects, not in bodies.

Extinction when a particular animal or plant has died out, never to be seen again.

Livestock animals raised on a farm or ranch, such as sheep or cattle.

Rural to do with the countryside, or a less populated area.

Scavenger someone or something that searches through garbage to find food, or some other useful item.

Savanna a flat grass plain with little or no trees.

Scrub low bushes or trees that cover a piece of ground.

Slums overcrowded, poor, and neglected area of housing in a town or city.

For More Information

Books

Bailey, Donna. Anna Sproule. *Kenya* (Where We Live). Chatham, NJ: Steck-Vaughn Library Division, 1991.

Dahl, Michael S. *Kenya*. Minneapolis, MN: Capstone, 1997.

Kagad, Falaq. Elizabeth Berg (Editor). *Kenya* (Festivals of the World). Milwaukee, WI: Gareth Stevens, 1997.

Video

Where in the World? *Kids Explore Kenya*. 1991.

Web Sites

An Introduction to Kenya

The country's history and culture—www.interknowledge.com.

Nairobi National Park

Explore the park—www.kenyaweb.com/tourism/parks/nairobi/nairobi.html.

Index